Pedro,

His Perro,

AND THE

Alphabet

Sombrero

Lynn Rowe Reed

HYPERION BOOKS FOR CHILDREN
NEW YORK

David

Text and illustrations © 1995 by Lynn Rowe Reed.
All rights reserved.
Printed in Singapore.
For information address Hyperion Books for Children,
114 Fifth Avenue, New York, New York 10011.
FIRST EDITION
1 3 5 7 9 10 8 6 4 2
Library of Congress Cataloging-in-Publication Data
Reed, Lynn Rowe.
Pedro, his perro, and the alphabet sombrero / Lynn Rowe Reed—1st ed.
p. cm.
Summary: When Pedro receives a fancy dog and a plain sombrero for
his birthday, he decides to make his hat as fancy as his dog with an
assortment of items listed alphabetically in Spanish.
ISBN 0-7868-0071-2 (trade)—ISBN 0-7868-2058-6 (lib. bdg.)
[1. Hats—Fiction.   2. Alphabet.   3. Spanish language materials—Bilingual.]   I. Title
PZ73.R38   1995   94-28215

The artwork for each picture is prepared using oil pastel on black Arches paper.
This book is set in 27-point Insignia.

For his birthday,
Pedro gets a perro
and a sombrero.

The dog is
very fancy.

But the hat is too plain.
So Pedro
and his perro fix it up.

avión

They add

bandera

cacto

A little more...

chimpancé

estrella

dulce

Air

gato

huevo

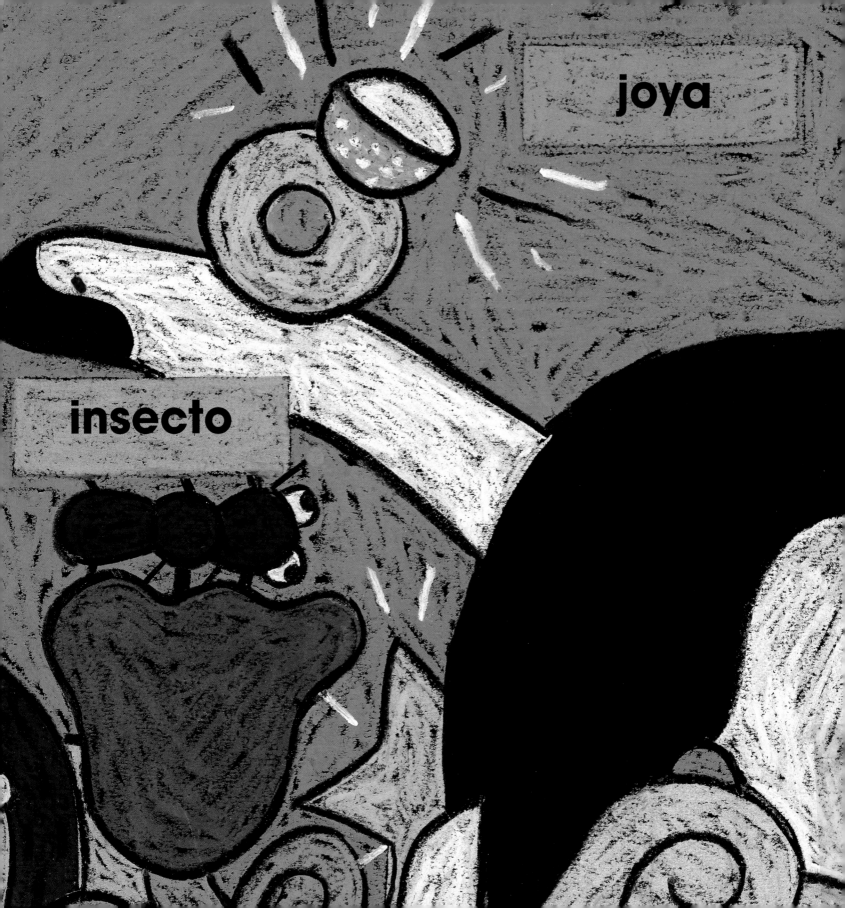

joya

insecto

kiwi

luna

nido

ñandú

The sombrero grows...

oruga

pez

queso

ratón

serpiente

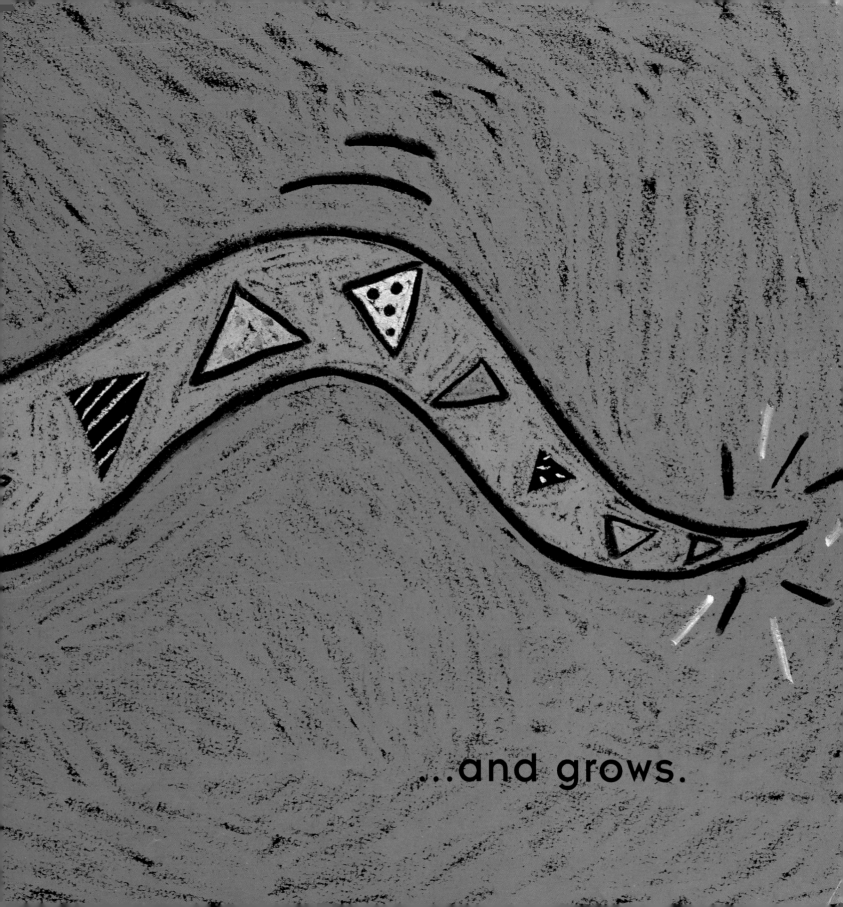

...and grows.

teléfono

¡Hola perro!

uvas

Get up, Pedro!

"Enough is enough,"
Pedro says.

But something else

wants to get
on Pedro's hat.

zorrillo

A note on the Spanish alphabet

Few Spanish words begin with the letters **k** and **x**. Those that do are often taken from other languages. **Kiwi**, for example, is a Maori word, now part of both the English and Spanish languages, while **xilófono** has its roots in Greek. Since **w** rarely appears in the Spanish language, no word beginning with the letter **w** was included.

Spanish has four additional letters, however: **ch**, **ll**, **ñ**, and **rr**. **Ñ** is rarely found at the beginning of a word; although **ñandú** is used when referring to the American ostrich, **avestruz** is more common. The rolling **r** sound—**rr**—is found only in the middle of words, as in **perro**.

GLOSSARY

adiós	good-bye	ah-**dyohs**	**nido**	nest	**nee**-doh
avión	airplane	ah-**vyohn**	**ñandú**	ostrich	**nyahn**-doo
bandera	flag	ban-**dehr**-ah	**oruga**	caterpillar	oh-**roo**-gah
cacto	cactus	**kahk**-toh	**perro**	dog	**peh**-rrow
chimpancé	chimpanzee	chim-pahn-**seh**	**pez**	fish	**pes**
dulce	candy	**dool**-seh	**queso**	cheese	**keh**-soh
estrella	star	es-**treh**-yah	**ratón**	rat	rah-**tohn**
flor	flower	**floor**	**serpiente**	snake	ser-**pyen**-tay
gato	cat	**gah**-toh	**sombrero**	hat	som-**breh**-roh
huevo	egg	**weh**-voh	**teléfono**	telephone	tel-**leh**-fon-oh
insecto	insect	in-**sek**-toh	**uvas**	grapes	**oo**-vahs
joya	jewel	**hoy**-ah	**violín**	violin	vee-oh-**leen**
kiwi	kiwi	**kee**-wee	**xilófono**	xylophone	zee-**loh**-foh-noh
luna	moon	**loo**-nah	**¡y se acaba!**	and it's done!	ee seh ah-**kah**-bah
llave	key	**yah**-veh		(or, more colloquially, that's it!)	
mariposa	butterfly	mah-rih-**poh**-sah	**zorrillo**	skunk	so-**ree**-yoh